MotorHead

Sheilah Prevost

MOTOR HEAD

By Sheilah Prevost

Published by:
Cedar Creek Press
3380 Terra Drive
Boise ID 83709

Acknowledgments

My heartfelt thanks to Rick Just who pushed me to assemble this collection of stories; John H. Donohue, M.D., skilled and kind surgeon; Brooks Potter, who literally took me for the ride of a lifetime; Cynthia Gibson, my daughter who accompanied me on the Big Ride weekend; Elizabeth, Clancy's caring and understanding nurse; Matt Orne,friend and Cirrus pilot and Tim Gibson, The Arranger.

This book is dedicated to “Coach”

Motor Head

I wanted to give Brooks a gift for his kind hospitality and I thought a box of cigars would fill the bill since he is a dedicated cigar smoker. I know that choice of cigar is a personal thing and we conferred, via e-mail, over the selection. With his advice, I went to the cigar store and bought a box of Monte Cristo Churchills. I had no idea that cigars are so expensive since this was my first foray into the cigar world. Brooks' delight was proportionate to the cost!

If you happened to be standing at Willow Springs International Motorsports Park, near the city of Lancaster, California, on a Tuesday last February, you would have observed the following: dry and scrubby land, the sun beating down on the hard track where the Porsches and BMWs and Ferraris tear around furiously, imminent danger, the pungent odor of hot grease in the pits and the shrieking sound of tires. You would have also seen a woman of a "certain age" zipped into a size 8 navy blue fire retardant racing suit, the kind that professional drivers wear, climbing inside a Porsche GT-3 Cup car, sporting an enormous grin.

That woman is me. This is the story of a motor head.

I'm a seventy-two year old widow and grandmother who has had a lifelong love affair with glamorous automobiles and who still possesses a need for speed. From the time I turned sixteen, with a newly acquired driver's license, my father, the Oldsmobile dealer in our small town in the mountains of Pennsylvania, always provided me with the latest sample from his inventory. As I look back, giving me the newest model to show off around town was a form of advertising for his business, not just a means of indulging his daughter. In any case, I appreciated his generosity. I didn't know, or care, about horsepower or engine dynamics. It was the *look* that I admired. The long sweep of the hood crowned by a deadly sharp ornament, the wide whitewall tires I labored to maintain in pristine condition with frequent scrubbings of Bon-Ami cleanser, a capacious trunk that accommodated a week's groceries—these features defined the cars, in my opinion.

I also confess that I was drawn more to the transportation of potential beaux than to their personal charms. A Thunderbird convertible could sway my heart faster than a bland four-door Dodge sedan. I classified my former boyfriends by their modes of transportation: a restored Model T Ford, a 1952 MG-TD, a British racing green Austin Healey, and for one date only, a decommissioned hearse. I find that now I'm unable to recall my suitors' appearances, but I still remember all their cars.

Besides three successive prosaic station wagons for hauling my kids around when they were growing up,

I've owned two 1953 MG-TDs, three Mazda RX-7s, and a "formerly owned" 1984 BMW 6-Series that I bought after selling a perfectly good Honda Accord with 30,000 miles on the clock. The BMW was perpetually in the shop with a variety of ailments but I loved the speed and profile of that noble lapis blue automobile. On an icy December morning in 2001 I was hit by a pickup truck, spun around three times, and smacked against a concrete barrier. My car was totaled. I rode to the salvage yard on the flatbed wrecker to retrieve the roundel from the hood. (It still rests on a bookshelf in my dining room twelve years later.) I had a boyfriend in college who, although a snoozer in all other respects, had a blue Jaguar saloon; his allure, besides the car, with its genuine burled walnut dashboard and fragrant leather seats, was that he took me to Watkins Glen International to watch the races.

Now I mostly drive a 2008 Mini Cooper S with 10,000 miles. My other car, safely harbored in the garage, is a sleek black 2007 BMW 335 XI with 29,000 miles. When I accelerate on the ramp leading up to the highway, my 335's gears shift like silk, eager to go faster. I'm on high alert for the state troopers as my car shows its stuff.

*

"Put your left foot in, then your butt, and pull yourself into the car," Dee said. I obeyed and squeezed into the Porsche GT-3 Cup car with no grace at all. My cheeks felt pleated in the carbon fiber helmet. Dee reached in, buckled and tightly cinched my five-point safety harness. He gave me a huge smile, and I returned a thumbs up with my gloved hand. Thumbs up or down are the universal language of racecar drivers, I was learning.

Brooks was behind the wheel, wearing his Nomex flame retardant suit, gloves, helmet, and red driving shoes. I wore tennis sneakers with my suit, helmet and gloves.

"Okay?"

"Yes," I said. "Let's do this."

"We'll take a lap around to see what you think."

I gave him the thumbs up. Brooks reached forward, activating several switches. I heard the whine of fuel pumps, noticed lights flashing on the instrument panel and felt air on my face from ducting on the dash. He keyed the starter and the Porsche's race engine immediately spoke in no uncertain terms. Clutching the car, Brooks eased it into first gear. We were off.

The Porsche was stripped of amenities, delivered this way directly from Porsche's racing facility in Weissach, Germany. This is a purpose-built race car, make no mistake: no back seat, a roll cage surrounding us, no padding on the interior of the doors, fire suppression cylinder on the floor. The plan was to take one easy lap and come back into the pit to see how I felt about things. Though it was loud and violent and I was slammed against the seat by the force of the Gs, I wasn't afraid. Swinging into the hot pits at the end of lap1, we were met by Dee and David, Brooks' techs. "Well," David said, "what do you think?" Brooks looked at me.

"Let's go again," I said. Brooks nodded. He said we would take the speed up a notch or two, which is exactly what we did.

*

So why, you may be wondering, would a retired fund-raising consultant and grandmother from Pennsylvania make the trek to California for, literally, the ride of a lifetime?

The genesis for the event was my viewing *The Bucket List*, a movie starring Jack Nicholson and Morgan Freeman, who, both seriously ill, share a hospital room. Each man has compiled a list of achievements to accomplish before dying. At the time I viewed the movie it didn't occur to me that I was about to embark on my own Bucket List although as I reflect on my activities over the past eighteen months, Bucket Listing appears to be what I've been doing. I learned to appreciate speed from my pilot husband, I guess. Once he was driving so fast on the ground, that I yelled, "Pull over! Pull over!" Shocked, he jammed on the brakes, asking, "What's the matter? Are you sick?" "No," I said. "It's too dangerous in the front seat. I'm getting in the back."

*

Brooks' hands were in perpetual motion, shifting, shifting. His feet flew over the pedals much like an organist pedaling a Bach *fugue.* The physicality required of a race car driver most likely is little known to observers. It is a symphony of vision, hands and feet in concert with complex mental processes. The driver is truly a predictor of *what is going to happen* before it actually does. Not unlike a jet pilot, the car's rate of closure on upcoming turns and obstacles requires the precise, predictive calculation of the driver. My late husband, an airline pilot who capped his career of 25 years as a captain of the 747-400, often spoke of "situational awareness" in the cockpit. Racing on the ground employs the same principle.

My first speed encounter occurred six months before my California adventure when I flew in a Cirrus. The Cirrus SR22 is a single-engine, four-seat composite airplane, built by Cirrus Aircraft with a 310 horsepower engine. It is equipped with CAPS, an emergency parachute capable of *lowering the entire aircraft (and occupants)* to the ground in an emergency, a comforting feature. A family friend, who is a real estate investor in Maine, offered to fly me to Portland from Pennsylvania to look over possible investment properties. Matt, the airplane owner and pilot, flew into our local airport to pick me up. Our airport is very small: one runway, no tower, a windsock and an Av-gas pump. Wheels up at 8 am. We flew the 337 miles to Portland in one hour and 51 minutes. The ride, at 11,000 feet, was thrilling as we broke through tiers of voluptuous clouds into the dazzling sunshine. Farms, highways, towns and windmill farms were easily visible from the cockpit. In the co-pilot seat, I wore a headset to dampen the noise and connect me to Matt via a voice-activated microphone. Maximum cruise speed of 211 knots (391 km/h). As we moved along, apparently effortlessly, I understood the glamor and excitement of flying one's own aircraft. It's surreal, the passenger (and pilot, too, I imagine) enjoying a near out-of-body experience. Had it been necessary to drive to Portland that day, the trip would have consumed nearly eight hours, compared to less than two hours in the Cirrus. I was back home again by dinner time.

*

Turn 9, at Willow Springs, has a long history of consuming cars and drivers. It's a very high-speed, off-camber, visually perplexing right hand sweeper leading onto the long front straightaway. If misjudged by the driver, the consequences are potentially fatal. This was the turn, I was told earlier, where things might get "interesting." The car, traveling north of 100 mph at turn entry, becomes light, drifting literally on the edge of adhesion. There is a very real possibility of becoming airborne. No problem, thanks to Brooks.

At the end of lap 3, the "next level," Brooks patted my knee reassuringly. My breakfast muffin and coffee were edging up in my gullet and my forehead was damp with sweat during lap 4 so when Brooks gave me a thumbs up for another lap, I responded with a flat hand signal. Brooks acknowledged with an exaggerated nod, and dropped the speed. We finished the lap and came in to the 18-wheeler transporter where his techs waited. Dee swung open my door, unbuckled my harness, and helped me out of the car. I stumbled once, recovered, handed him my helmet and walked behind the Evosport Engineering rig to an empty 50-gallon oil drum and threw up—twice. At our top speed, we had reached 144 miles per hour.

Brooks Potter is a principal in Evosport Engineering, a company in Huntingdon Beach, California that engineers performance products for Mercedes, BMW, Porsche and Ferrari. In addition, and specific to Brooks' passion, they build and service race cars. Six feet tall, with dark hair and eyes, at 55 he retains the easy grace of the college athlete who played center midfield in Division 1 lacrosse. When he drives, Brooks is completely focused on the business at hand. He has won 4 SCCA National titles and he captured the Pirelli Drivers Cup championship in 2010.

His partner, John Trefethen, is a fellow racer and patriarch of Trefethen Vineyards in Napa Valley. They first "met" at the outside of Laguna Seca's turn 11 in a Pirelli Driver's Cup race. The two became close friends and even closer racers. In 2011, they joined forces and began building a team at Evosport Engineering.

So when Brooks offered a ride on a racetrack in California, I jumped at the chance to go fast in a fast car. I was becoming a speed junky.

I flew to Los Angeles on Thursday, February 21st. My daughter, Cynthia, met me and we checked into the Beverly Wilshire. Early the following morning the temperature was 68 degrees and the California sun was alluring as we drove 80 miles to Willow Springs International Motorsports Park. As we progressed further north, trailer parks and worn houses dotted the landscape, a stark contrast to the lush environs of Beverly Hills.

At the track, the Evosport Engineering tractor-trailer was parked next to the Porsche GT-3 we would use. Nearby was the stunning $600,000 hand-built race car, Evosport's new World Challenge entry, Number 24, the Mercedes Benz. The car had an aura all its own. Sensuous fenders hugged the body. The windshield swept back to the roof in a delicious arc. Magnificent!

After our lapping session, Cynthia, Brooks and I (still in my Nomex suit and feeling pretty good about life) lounged under the awning on the side of the big rig. He turned on his video camera to interview me when Cynthia leaned into the lens, saying, "I always knew Mom was a Motor Head."

I agree.

Dead End

Ada County, in upper New York State, never was a bustling area. Most of the men in the county work construction three hours away in Syracuse from April until late fall. November finds them in the unemployment line, signing up for weekly checks to keep their families from starving until the weather breaks in the spring. Freezing winters are consumed with TV watching, drinking cheap beer and yelling at their wives.

Outside Greensboro, the county seat, on the winding blacktop road to Nirvana Lake, dirt lanes fork off to rustic cottages built in the 1920s. In warm weather frogs hop about on the rainy nights, frolicking toward death as the next car approaches, their lives terminated with a *squish*. Cottages, some with outhouses, traditionally are handed down in families since there is scant demand for real estate on Nirvana. Third generation owners, many of whom have left for good and made their way to New York City or Toronto or Philadelphia, rarely return to the lake. It's too long a drive, for one thing. Why spend five or six hours on bad roads only to end up at a dreary lake where it rains every day? Black flies swarm in July and August. The laundromat and grocery store are 40 minutes away. Modern families want shopping malls, motels with in-ground pools and entertainment for the kids.

Marcus Franklin was the sole exception to the migration away from the lake. Three months earlier he had moved from Rochester into his inherited cottage with no plans other than painting the trim on the windows. The environment suited him. He relished the silence, occasionally paddling the Old Town canoe on the tiny lake or smoking a cheap cigar on the dock. Once again out of work, he determined he wouldn't try again. All of his previous attempts at joining the corporate world during the past twenty years had ended in humiliation. No employer complained that he didn't work hard. In fact, he went to the office early and stayed to the end of the day. The problem was that he couldn't get along with colleagues, his peers, or his superiors either. There was also the issue of communication. When things were going badly, he couldn't bring himself to talk about the problems. In stressed times he walked heavily and his sluggish cadence of speech slowed even more, punctuated by occasional angry outbursts. Once again, he had earned pariah status; he was fired. In his last position he managed the final production in a hearing aid plant, where, distracted by what he knew was another impending dismissal, he suffered the humiliation of shipping five thousand devices out the door with the critical components missing. Every single device was returned to dealers accompanied by abusive letters, nearly destroying the proud 75-year old company.

With a modest income from bonds from his father's estate, augmented by unemployment compensation, he could survive if he lived frugally. His twelve-year old Chevrolet was paid for, he rarely bought new clothes, he could afford the moderate taxes on the cottage and he ate sparingly. His only indulgence was an occasional solitary dinner out when he journeyed to Syracuse or over the Canadian border.

Marcus's half-log cabin suited his penny-pinching ways. Cracked linoleum covered the floor of the three rooms downstairs, the ancient furnace hissed and sputtered, emitting more noise than heat, and the mismatched relics of furniture, with sprung seats and frayed coverings, were family leftovers from earlier days. Upstairs, the flaccid mattress on the double bed dumped the occupant to the middle every night.

During his undergraduate years at Jenkins College, Marcus frequently enjoyed the company of women who attended nearby schools. He was a good-looking man, six feet tall and fit, the only child of an aggressive, razor-tongued trial attorney. Marcus was never much of a talker but girls liked his silence; they often interpreted his stillness as waters running deep. In fact, he said little because he had little to say. He didn't think about others much. Curiosity was not in his repertoire. Introspection and analysis were foreign to him. Early on he cultivated a drawl to mask his slow mind; speaking slowly, in his case, indicated thinking slowly. At least he was smart enough to recognize that.

Marcus's one foray into matrimony ended badly. During his senior year at Jenkins, he courted Betsy Davis, a sweet-faced blonde who was a student at nearby Cornell. She admired Marcus' physique and his little red convertible and before she knew it she was skipping down the aisle of St. Paul's Episcopal in the company of three hundred guests. During the reception at the country club, a discomfiting scene ensued between the new bridegroom and his father-in-law.

"You have enough money with you?"

"Well, sir, I have five hundred dollars," Marcus said.

"Five hundred? What the hell. You need more than that to take this trip to Hawaii," Gregory Davis said. "What's wrong with you?"

"Nothing, sir. I thought Betsy could pay her share."

"Pay her share? My god, boy, she's your wife now. You're supposed to take care of her." Mr. Davis opened his wallet and jammed seven one hundred dollar bills into his new son-in-law's pocket.

Pleased, Marcus extended his hand to Mr. Davis. "Thanks a lot." Mr. Davis turned away.

Doomed from the start, the marriage lasted a brief year. After Betsy's miscarriage, she returned to her father's house. Divorce papers were filed immediately. Marcus did not attempt marriage again.

The sting of the failed marriage severely affected him. Within a decade his looks deteriorated to grizzled roughness as his cheeks sagged and his eyes disappeared into the folds of his lids. His resonant tenor voice turned reedy. His shoulders rounded and his derriere flattened. He was an old man at 44 when he finally gave up and moved to the lake.

The tick-tick-tick of the sticky valve lifters preceded the vehicle by 100 yards. Dust swirled on the unpaved road as the bulbous black hearse with the cracked vinyl top waddled into view. Ignition off, the engine continued, dieseling, finally ceasing. The door opened and a scrawny man wearing tuxedo pants and a sparkling white shirt emerged. His hair was thick with shiny pomade. His bowed legs could accommodate a small animal's passage. Brown tobacco-stained fingers tossed a Camel on the ground.

"This here's the Jackson place?"

"What do you want?" Marcus asked. "You're on private property."

"Yeah, well, no offense, Mister. I'm lookin' for Amos Jackson."

"I don't know who you're talking about. I said this is private property. You'd better leave."

"Hey, man, you don't need to get huffy with me. I ain't committed no crime or nothing. I'm just a guy tryin' to earn a living. Amos Jackson told me he lived around here. You sure this ain't his place?"

"Look," Marcus said. "I told you. There's no Jackson here or on the lake as far as I know. Why are you driving that hearse? Are you an undertaker?"

"Hell, no, man. This here's my business car." The man lit another Camel. "What you doin' up here this time of year? Most folks have left the lake by now. You live here all year?"

"Yes, I live here. Alone. And I like it that way."

"Oh, yeah? You work or anything?"

Marcus stared at the man. "No, I don't work. Any more. I'm retired."

"No kidding. You rich or something? How come you ain't working?"

Marcus stiffened. "It's none of your business."

"Well, hell, I don't mean to offend. But, you know, if you ever want some work, I could help you out. Always lookin' for drivers. Yessir, always looking."

The man got back in the hearse, started the engine and rolled down the window. He extended his hand toward Marcus. "Lissen, this here's my business card. I live in Greensboro. You change your mind, give me a call." The card drifted from his hand to the lawn. With a puff of exhaust, the hearse rumbled down the road. Marcus shrugged and went inside the cabin.

A week later, as Marcus was eating his usual fare of baked beans and hot dogs, a roar, followed by an explosion, burst from the utility room. Opening the door, Marcus found the ancient gas furnace throwing off sparks; smoke filled the space. Two brief sputters, then stillness. Overnight, the outside temperature dropped to the mid-20s. When Marcus arose the next morning his neck was stiff and his joints ached. Frost outlined the window panes. He went to the telephone and called Morgan Brothers Heating and Plumbing in Greensboro.

Avery Morgan alighted from his truck, remembering his childhood days when Marcus, the city snob, called him a hick and a dope. He tapped the defunct furnace with his wrench.

"Shot to hell," Avery said.

"Can you fix it?"

"Nope, sorry, Mark. This system's at least forty years old. You got your money's worth, that's for sure. Guess you have to bite the bullet or freeze your ass off." He smiled as he delivered the bad news."I have to think about this."

"Suit yourself." Avery climbed into his pickup.

Later that morning, as Marcus entered the Val-You parking lot, the exhaust pipe on his ancient faded red car crashed on the macadam with a scraping clatter. Opening the door, he peered beneath the auto, examining the damage. He leaned against the fender, arms crossed, head down.

"Jesus Christ, what the hell is happening? First the furnace, now the car. What am I going to do?"

He spotted the ancient hearse parked in front of the hardware store. Walking over, he saw the pomaded driver on the front seat. The man said, "Everything all right?"

"No, it isn't."

" You in trouble?"

"What are you trying to do, rub it in?"

"Listen, Mister. You look like you could use some work."

"Yes," Marcus said, humbled. "I could."

"Well," said the driver, extending his hand. "My name's Georgie Williams and like I said, I need drivers. You interested?

"I might be. What do you pay and where do they drive?"

"Two fifty a round trip to Canada. Twice a week."

"What's the reason for the trip?"

"Look," Williams said. "'At's my business. My drivers keep their mouths shut and don't ask questions. I pay every Friday. Come out to my house this afternoon."

The red brick house with shiny black shutters perched at the top of the winding driveway. The lush lawn was mowed and edged; blue hydrangeas bloomed by the front steps. A red barn was visible in the back lot. A slim blonde woman, wearing pink and green silk pants and a pink twinset, stood on the front porch. Fat pearls looped between her breasts. She was smoking a cigarette in a long black holder. "What do you want?" she said.

"Georgie said he'd hire me."

"When?"

"Today. At the Val-You. I'm Marcus Franklin."

"Oh, you the new driver?"

"Yes," Marcus said.

"What did he tell you?" She twirled her pearls with tanned hands.

"Not much," Marcus said. "He just said the trip is a round trip, back and forth to Canada. He pays on Fridays."

"Did he tell you you're supposed to keep your mouth shut?"

"Yes, something like that."

"Look at me," she said. "Look right at me and pay attention."

"What?"

"You heard me," she said. "This is important. I'll say it once. Get that?"

Marcus looked at the woman. She nodded at him. "Remember what I say. You keep your goddamn mouth shut." She pointed her finger at him.

"Yes, ma'am," Marcus said.

"Okay. Go out back. Georgie's waiting for you." She went into the house, the screen door slamming behind her. Marcus went to the back yard.

Georgie opened the door on the driver's side of the hearse, motioning for Marcus to get in. "Guess you met the little woman."

"She's your wife?"

"Hey, man, she's got the class in this family. I take orders from her," Georgie said. "Okay, you're all loaded up. Follow the map. I expect you back by midnight."

He handed the map to Marcus, the route highlighted in yellow.

"Wait a minute. You want me to start out now?"

"You bet, Mister. Get your ass in the car."

"I thought I would start next week."

"Look, you need the job or not?"

"All right, all right. What about stopping for coffee?"

"Yeah, once up and once back." Marcus drove off.

Ten miles down the road he pulled over, cutting the ignition. He leaned his forehead on the steering wheel. Looking up, he snapped his fingers and got out. At the back of the vehicle, he turned the handle on the door. Inside, an ebony coffin with silver handles was secured to the floor with webbing and three padlocks. It seemed genuine. But who could know? He returned to the driver's seat, started the hearse and drove a mile, stopping at an intersection. He looked to the left and to the right. Making his decision, he turned the car around.

Georgie was waiting for him at the top of the driveway.

"Always the same," he said. "Cold feet get you?"

"Look," Marcus said. "I don't know what's in here but I've got a bad feeling. I can't do this."

"Okay by me," Williams said. "Guess you's a man of leisure and don't need the money. That's okay. There's more fish in the sea." He winked.

"Drugs? Is that what I'm driving?"

Williams spat on the ground. "What do you think is going on here, rich boy? You think I'm some kind of dope runner? Don't you know 'bout the border guards? How they look at your cargo?"

"I just thought..."

"Don't think. You want the work or not?"

The screen door slammed and Williams' wife strode into the yard. "Well, Mr. Marcus Franklin, aren't you the big shot," the woman said. "Georgie, I told you, this one's too scared to drive. He's chicken shit. Get rid of him."

"No, no, I need the work. I'll take the load." The furnace payments loomed and there was his crippled car. Marcus climbed back into the hearse. He started the engine. Georgie and his wife watched as he drove away.

South on 11, west on 812 to Ogdensburg. At the border, the uniformed guard held up his hand, palm forward.

"Where are you going, sir?"

" Abbottsville." The town marked on the map.

"Yes sir. And the purpose of your visit?"

"I'm making a delivery to the funeral home."

"How long will you be staying?"

"I won't. It's a turnaround trip."

The guard peered in the back window of the hearse, nodded, and motioned Marcus through. Marcus felt the sweat run in thin rivers down his back. Was this only a close call and the guard would snag him on the way back?

Over the next forty miles, shabby houses and two trailer parks dotted the sides of the road. Battered, abandoned vehicles rusted in the fields. In the clearing beyond, the crossroads on the map became reality. The Macartney General Store was on the left, Macartney Funeral Home on the right. Parking under the porte cochere, Marcus rang the bell. An old man with a gray ponytail opened the door.

"What's up, Sonny?"

"I'm Georgie Williams' driver."

"Oh, right. Come on in. We'll give you a cup of coffee while we unload. Cream and sugar?"

"No, black."

Marcus rested on the settee in the foyer. The place seemed genuine; potted palms occupied the corners of the waiting area, folding chairs filled the room to the left. Organ music drifted through the speakers on the wall. The man with the ponytail brought coffee. "Black, right?"

"Thanks." Marcus sipped the strong brew. "Say, you know what my cargo is?"

Scowling, the man said, "Here's some advice, Sonny. Mind your own business and you won't get in trouble. Want to use the can before you leave? It's in there." He pointed toward the back.

The four-hour return drive was unremarkable. A new border guard asked where Marcus was born, yawned while he answered and waved him over the border. By the time he hit Greensboro, Marcus' back was bent with fatigue. He nodded as Williams told him to come back on Thursday for another trip.

A routine was established. Twice weekly, Marcus reported to work, drove his unknown cargo to Macartney's, and returned. Georgie was as good as his word—he paid every Friday. Marcus established a payment plan with Morgan Plumbing and Heating and the furnace in the cabin was replaced, although the exhaust on the Chevrolet still needed work. Marcus began to enjoy his routine. No one criticized his work, he knew when he was finished, he didn't need to deal with many people, there was no issue of not getting along. For him, it was the ideal situation. The sole question in his mind was identification of his cargo. His mind returned to the question occasionally the way a bothersome tooth demands a probing tongue.

On Tuesday of the fourth week, Marcus drove up to the house to find Georgie standing next to a coffin in the driveway. "My other guy didn't show up. You got to help me lift this bugger," Georgie said. The two men struggled with the box, dropping it once on the driveway.

"Pick it up, pick it up," Georgie shouted.

As the box slid in the opening, Marcus wiped his face. "I can't believe a dead body weighs that much."

"That wood is real heavy," Georgie said. "Okay, I'll just fasten the locks and you get on your way."

Georgie's wife slammed the door behind her. She waved her cigarette in Marcus' face. "What's the matter, rich man? You look all tired out. Can't do the job?"

"I can do it, all right. Leave me alone." Marcus started the hearse and drove down the driveway. His forehead was lined with worry.

At Ogdensburg, a new guard stopped him. "What's in the back?"

"I'm making a delivery to Macartney's in Abbotsville. Routine."

"Yeah? Open up. I want to see what's in there." The guard peered in the hearse. "Unlock the padlocks."

"I don't have the keys. I'm only the driver." Marcus turned his pockets inside out, nervous. "I told you, I'm only the driver."

"Look, mister, I don't care who you are." He leaned close to the coffin. "This thing stinks. What's in there?"

"It's going to Macartney's to be cremated. Dead bodies have a tendency to smell, sir." Pleased with himself for his creativity, Marcus smiled.

"Yeah? What are you smiling about, Buster?"

"Look, I don't have the key. I can't do anything for you. Search the hearse if you don't believe me."

The guard's face was close to his for a long moment. He reeked of beer and sweat. "All right, get out of here." He waved Marcus through the crossing.

Georgie met him at the top of the driveway. "What in hell's goin' on here, Marcus? How come you're two hours late?"

"I had to come through the Hopkinton crossing because the Ogdensburg guard was suspicious about the coffin. I was scared to come back through the same way."

"Damn."

"Yeah, well, what about me? I could be in jail--or worse."

"That's it. No more work for a week. Maybe more," Georgie said. "We got to let things cool off. I'll get in touch with you."

"But I thought this was a regular job," Marcus said. "I need the money."

"Keep your shirt on, buddy. It is what it is. Go home. I'll be in touch."

Over the next six days Marcus puttered around the dock, brought the flowerpots and chairs into the boathouse. He scraped the peeling paint on the windows. He paced the living room in the evenings. Georgie arrived on Friday, the hearse burping and belching smoke as he drove in.

"Okay. Things is all set. You're back to work, rich man. Interested?"

"You fixed it?"

"Be at my house Tuesday after lunch." Georgie drove off.

As Marcus neared the Ogdensburg border, leading a line of seven cars, he spied three more vehicles ahead of him, stopped for a meticulous search by guards who were foraging through the trunks of their cars. The owners were standing outside, shuffling their feet, obviously annoyed. What the hell? The lazy guards were apparently looking for something in particular. Distracted by the threat of discovery, Marcus drove off the road onto the berm. The hearse skidded on the dirt toward the culvert, brakes locking as he attempted to return to the macadam. The elderly vehicle tilted to the right, nearly capsizing. He over-twisted the wheel, creating a left-hand list. The hearse tumbled onto its side with a thunderous *crack*. The coffin smashed free of the locks and webbing, skidding sideways. The lid slammed the front seat as it was liberated from the box. Something bony flew through the air, striking Marcus on his face. It was a desiccated finger. In fright and disgust, Marcus vomited on his lap.

The back door flew open, the coffin slewed out of the vehicle, slamming on the ground with a deafening *thwack*. The putrid skeletal body levitated into the air, falling to the road, freeing packs and packs of hidden thousand dollar bills. Canvas bags of glittering gold South African Krugerrands burst open against the hood of the car behind Marcus. The bounty flew into the air, coming to rest on the road. Drivers in the other cars leapt out to retrieve the reeking money, charging into each other in their frenzy.

They seized all of the bills and the gold, raced to their cars and sped off.

The guards grabbed Marcus, handcuffed him and drove to the local jail where they charged him with reckless behavior since all of the evidence had been removed by the other drivers. His 10' by 10' cell was furnished with a cot, lumpy mattress and a foul pillow. In the corner was an open toilet.

Marcus phoned Georgie's house from jail. The female voice said, "He's not here. He's out of the country and he's not coming back." Panicky, Marcus called again. "I'm in jail, Mrs. Georgie," he shrieked. "You have to help me. They won't let me out."

"This is a wrong number," she said. "Don't call back." The line went dead.

The empty hearse was towed to the auto graveyard. Macartney's Funeral Home scooped up the human remains. Marcus languished in prison for more than five weeks until the authorities figured out he had no funds to pay a fine or hire a lawyer. When released, Marcus had four dollars in his pocket. He began to walk south to the border and the guards waved him through. Marcus walked for two days, occasionally raising his thumb at passing cars, none of which would pick up the dirty bearded man. About thirty miles from the lake, he stopped at a general store.

"Get outta here, Mister. I don't want any bums in my store," said the owner.

"But, sir, I only want to buy a soda."

"Go somewhere else."

Finally, he returned to the lake, exhausted. To his delight, when he entered the cottage, the new furnace was still working. "I'm just a lucky guy," he said to himself as he took a beer from the fridge and lit a cheap cigar.

George Plimpton Shaved Here

In the early 1980s in Syracuse, New York after nine grueling interviews, I landed the position of General Manager of the University Club. Only months before my arrival, club by-laws were rewritten to admit women members, a move engendered by the possible loss of tax-exempt status. The law may have forced them to admit women; they didn't have to like it and they viewed me as a symbol of all that was wrong with modern times.

My euphoria over the new job quickly dissipated upon learning that most of the older members hated the idea of my being there. My predecessor, Hal, was a man who held the job for more than a quarter of a century. He played bridge with the members at noon, sipped cocktails with them at the end of the day and, best of all, he never replaced the draperies or moved the furniture in the library. During the latter years of his tenure the interior of the club took on a frayed, musty appearance as the clubhouse deteriorated with age and inattention. In the members' eyes, this was to Hal's credit since no assessments were levied to cover the cost of replacing the shabby furnishings, the ancient furnace or worn-out kitchen equipment

In the minds of the Old Guard, I was an interloper, an invader come to wreak change in their sanctuary away from wives and secretaries. It didn't help that I was the first woman manager in the history of the 75-year old club either. Under my predecessor's direction the same waitresses served the same members the same sandwich every day. No matter that housekeeping was slovenly, bartenders were drinking on the job, houseboys were smoking weed on the roof and the bookkeeper embezzled $30,000; at least the old gentlemen saw the same faces every day when they arrived for lunch.

During that first year I fired half the staff, re-arranged the furniture and eventually convinced the directors to impose a loathsome assessment to save their aging Georgian building. I also placed camphor blocks in the smelly urinals and inadvertently walked in on a judge who was dressing in the locker room. It seemed that whatever I did, it was the wrong thing. Many members referred to me as "she" as in "Things were a lot better around here before *she* arrived."

During my second tumultuous year, in an effort to offer a positive experience to the members, I decided to reinstate a long-abandoned club tradition: the annual Father/Son banquet. Yellowed press clippings yielded information that traditionally the evening's speaker was a sports figure from nearby Syracuse University— the Athletic Director or a coach, for example. Why, I mused, couldn't we import an internationally known sportsman/ raconteur who would add panache to the occasion? It should be someone from a larger world, I thought, someone with humor and flair. Discussion of choice of speaker with one of my handful of supporters produced George Plimpton's name. I knew about Mr. Plimpton from his gig as the triangle player with the New York Philharmonic and was vaguely aware of his participatory sports journalism. Perhaps he could be the man to thaw the ossified members.

A trip to the public library yielded the appropriate Manhattan telephone number. When I spoke to the youngish-sounding assistant and presented my case, he said Mr. Plimpton's fee for a dinner engagement was $5,000 plus expenses, a monumental sum for a club hovering on the brink of insolvency. I pleaded and whined, begging for a reduction. Eventually the phone call came; Mr. Plimpton would speak for $3,000 plus expenses. Agreed. We set the date for late September. Now all I needed was to raise the money.

As it turned out, five local stockbrokers and one banker anted up $500 each. Another banker donated airfare and hotel accommodations. In each case when I approached these CEOs their reaction was nearly the same: "George Plimpton? He's the guy who played with the Detroit Lions. Great idea—I'll send you a check." Evidently Plimpton's Mitty-esque exploits in the arena demonstrated a virtuosity none of these men would ever achieve but which they greatly admired. The evening sold out quickly.

When he stepped off the airplane, his rangy figure was clad in gray flannels, a wrinkled shirt and rumpled seersucker jacket (well past the Labor Day deadline for such summer wear) and his loafers were scuffed. The familiar shock of gray hair drifted over his brow. A clean blue shirt and shaving kit were under his arm. As he lowered himself into the front seat of my MG-TD, he remarked in that indefinable trans-Atlantic accent, "Great car. One summer four of us motored through Spain in a car like this."

As we drove along the airport road I asked him about Jean Stein's recent book, *Edie*, which he edited. Edie Sedgwick was a beautiful young member of Andy Warhol's "factory." Her brief life was fraught with fleeting fame, drugs and alcohol. Sadly, she died at 28.

"Yes, poor girl," Mr. Plimpton said. "She extinguished herself," a gentle term for suicide which I silently adopted.

Nearing town, he asked, "Is there some place where I can shave and change my shirt?"

"Certainly," I said. "I'll take you to the house. It's on the way to the club."

"Great. By the way, call me George."

At the house I showed him to the second floor, pointing out the bathroom and bedroom where he could change while I waited downstairs. He returned shortly, tossing the dirty shirt and shaving gear into the back seat. Off we drove.

The evening, by any measure, was a great success. During cocktails, the brokers and bankers and dentists and accountants crowded around George, bombarding him with questions about his adventures. He graciously answered with self-deprecating humor and you never would have known he probably had heard the same questions dozens, perhaps hundreds, of times before. Even the Old Guard arrived, their curiosity intact and their disapproval of me parked at the door.

After dinner, while the members puffed their Cubans and Macanudos, George told his tales with gusto. His delivery was fresh and the members and their sons howled with amusement as he told about tackles on the field and humiliating encounters in the ring. He told us that Leonard Bernstein fired him from the New York Phil and re-hired him almost immediately. Questions followed and the evening ended with a standing ovation.

We drove to his hotel in the cool night air. He appeared pleased with the proceedings and declined my offer of a lift to the airport in the morning, saying he would take a cab. I handed him an envelope with his check; we shook hands and I drove home.

In the bathroom sink I discovered his whiskers and his shirt cardboard was on the bed. I collected the whiskers, placed them in a plastic bag and, together with the cardboard, stashed the articles in my sweater drawer. Years later, when moving to Washington, D.C., I found the cache and took it with me. When I moved to Boise, Idaho the bag traveled along with my other possessions. My final move to Pennsylvania in 2000 also included the "George" bag. It was only when he died suddenly in September 2003 that I took out the bag and cardboard and cremated the contents in the fireplace.

I wish I could say the Plimpton evening was a turning point and the Old Guard relented, that the following day they greeted me with enthusiasm and courtesy. In fact, that isn't the case. However, the détente had begun and through the following months, continued. At one point I overheard the afore-mentioned judge comment to a colleague, "You know, she's not so bad." High praise. Over the next five years we all came to a tacit accord. When I resigned in 1987, the members feted me with a send-off party and a generous gift. No small thing, indeed. Thanks, George.

Night Flight

"My husband died this morning."

A woman wearing a jean jacket embellished with sequins and red satin ribbon trim on the collar took the vacant seat next to me. Her black leather pants cupped her toned derriere. Her ankle-high lizard boots sparkled; nails and hair were freshly done. Most likely, she was on the good side of sixty although it was difficult to tell. We were in the waiting area of Gate F19 in the Minneapolis-St. Paul airport along with dozens of other weary travelers waiting to go to Detroit.

Stunned, I looked at her. "Pardon?" I said.

"Yes, it's true. We were in San Diego. I nearly missed my flight after my hair appointment."

I remember my inertia after my husband died. I could barely function and the thought of going to the hairdresser was the last possible thing I could have managed.

It was nearly 7 pm on a Friday. Up since dawn, I had been trying to travel since 6:30 that morning when I left the hotel in Boise. Finally I snagged a seat on the 2 p.m.

flight to Minneapolis. My day fell apart after that. Bounced from three flights so far, my patience was gossamer-thin. My clothes were wrinkled and my makeup was tired. I felt as though I was the "before" in a makeover ad.

The preceding week had been a nightmare. My Boise consulting client had expressed severe displeasure with the lack of progress on the museum's capital campaign. Two major donors had threatened to renege on their pledges. After meeting with both prospects, I felt as though their gifts were salvageable but only time would tell. I was ready to go home.

"I'm leaving for the tennis court," I called.

Clancy came to the front door to say goodbye. "I like your little tennis skirt," he said. "You still have those killer legs. Remember...?

I knelt to tighten the laces on my white Adidas sneakers, eyeing his red Jack Purcells. "I know what you're going to say."

"Fort Lauderdale," he said. "I told you I would know those legs anywhere."

"It wouldn't have worked," I said.

"Sure it would and we wouldn't have wasted all those years."

I stood, smoothing my skirt. "I had responsibilities and so did you."

He patted my cheek, a familiar gesture. "Man, you sure were prissy."

"I was just trying to do the right thing—a husband, kids at home. You were married, *Clancy."*

"Yeah, well, I wasn't a fanatic about it," he said, laughing.

"It wasn't funny." I felt my face tighten. "Although I must confess I liked your style," I said.

"You always did the right thing in school—student council, yearbook, all that stuff."

"Those things were important to me."

"Yeah, I guess so. I had a lot more fun."

"Blowing up Mr. Jacob's mailbox, for instance?"

"That was great," he said. "But I sure caught hell from Dad."

"And all your wives."

"I got it right with you."

Smiling, I kissed his cheek. "Got to go."

"So long, Killer."

March is spring-break month, flights were oversold, and business travelers were trying to get home for the weekend. As a pilot's spouse, I was flying on standby status and the large crowd in the waiting area made me nervous. The problem was that all paying passengers would get a seat before those of us flying "Non-Rev." If only I could get on the flight to Detroit, I could stay overnight at the Airport Westin.

"I rode here in First Class from San Diego, right up next to the pilots," she said. "Wasn't that nice?"

"Was your husband ill?" Her "Opium" perfume was in the air.

"Oh, yes, for six months. That cancer, you know, it's *bad*. He was in hospice in Detroit, but two weeks ago I took him to California. I thought he should see the west," she said.

I remembered the grinding pain my husband endured for nearly three years. Time between surgeries provided some relief but always, in the back of our minds, was the specter of recurrence. I thought about the early morning telephone call from the Mayo Clinic. His voice was ragged and weary.

"They told me I have cancer," he said.

"Cancer?"

"Yes, my bellyache turns out to be a tumor," he said.

"I thought everything was all right. I thought they took care of your burst appendix and there wasn't anything else to take care of," I said.

"Yeah, me too. Guess not."

"Did he enjoy the trip?" I asked.

"Well, he didn't see much, what with the pain and morphine and oxygen and all." I caught a whiff of vodka.

"His daughter, Melodee (she emphasized the final syllable) was so *mean* to me. I took care of Archie for two years. I loved that man, and he loved me. Anyway, you know what Melodee said after he passed? She said, 'I hope Daddy goes to heaven to be with my *mother* where he belongs.' Can you imagine?" She ran her hands through her lightly-frosted hair and examined her nails.

"After Archie passed, I ran my hands over his thin body. I talked to him and asked him to look after me. I thanked him for the insurance policies." She paused. "Did you know you can get life insurance when you're old? Archie did." She smiled. "Anyway, then I called Archie's best friends, all four of them. I told them Archie had passed and did they want to talk to him?"

The shock must have shown on my face. "They talked to him?"

"Oh, yes. One said a prayer. Another just said, 'Goodbye, Archie.' I thought calling them was a nice touch, don't you?" She frowned. "One said he thought I was a crazy broad to do such a thing. But that's Wilbur. I say, consider the source. Wilbur never was much of a fan of mine."

"I told the undertaker I didn't want my Archie put in one of those black plastic bags with the noisy zipper," she said. "So they wrapped him in a nice white sheet when they took him out. It was the least I could do, don't you think?"

As she carefully mopped her tears, I noticed her mascara stayed in place. "My name is Janie. What's yours?"

"Sheilah," I said.

"Well, Sheilah, let me tell you something about insurance. Two years ago when Archie and I got married, I told him I wanted him to take proper care of me. So he bought all that insurance. Can you believe it? At his age—he was seventy-five—he bought those policies. I thank the good Lord that he did." She smiled. "I sat next to the nicest man on the flight from San Diego. He understood what I was going through and he was so helpful." She dug in her purse. "Here—look, he gave me his card. He said his wife died, too. He's going to call me and help me get through this. He said we should go to a new restaurant in Bloomfield Hills that he wants to try."

"Hey, how about going out for dinner this weekend? There's a new restaurant on the Beach that sounds like fun," Billy said. "I'm calling from my new Mercedes convertible. You would really like this car."

"Billy, I can't. I wouldn't be any fun. It's nice of you to ask, but I just can't."

"Listen, you need to get out. You can't just stay in and brood. There's a whole world out there. We'd have a good time," he said.

The thought of having dinner with another man didn't tempt me in the least. I wanted to eat oatmeal or yogurt at home, alone.

"When is Archie's funeral?" I asked.

Once, when I was sitting by Clancy's bed in the hospital, feeling as though he was going to die, I decided to make a list of pallbearers for his funeral. I spent nearly an hour on the list and then placed it in my handbag. Later, after we returned home, one evening we were in a neighborhood restaurant and I offered to pay the check. As I pulled my credit card from my bag, the list fell on the floor. I scooped it up hastily.

"What's that?"

"Oh, nothing," I said.

"No, what is it? Can I see it?"

"Well, if you must know, it's a list of pallbearers," I said.

"For me?"

"Yes. I thought you were going to die after this last operation."

Clancy scrutinized the list, nodding as he went through the names. "Well, you've got some good ones here. Pilots, our friend in the FBI, neighbors. I'm not sure about your brother, though."

"Oh, come on," I said. "His feelings would be hurt."

"Yeah, I guess that's true," he said.

When the time came, I called the entire list. Everyone accepted.

"Well, dear, I don't know. I left him there in California. That daughter of his can take care of those details. She is so bossy. I can't deal with all that."

"So you won't attend?"

"You know, Sheilah, I already said goodbye to Archie. Now I'm going back to sort through the furniture and stuff in the Bloomfield Hills house. That daughter of his owns it but Archie wrote it down that I can stay there for a year. That's enough time for me to put things in storage, clean out the place and take care of the paperwork. After I do that, I'm going to travel. Maybe go on a cruise."

"I can't do this anymore," he said. I'm sick and tired of being sick and tired. I hate the trips to the emergency room and the surgeries. I hate the vomiting and pain and all the other goddamn parts of being sick. This is too hard on me and on you."

"I hate this conversation," I said.

"There's no point in living like this. Hell, it isn't living," he said.

I looked at his gaunt frame, thirty pounds less than a year ago. His mouth turned down at the corners. His eyes, once bright and alluring, were clouded and pale.

The crowd had grown; all seats in the waiting area were occupied. Luggage blocked the aisles; newspapers littered the floor. As they surrounded the podium, passengers were shuffling their feet like horses at the starting gate. The harried agent kept her head down, focused on her computer. Reluctantly, she looked up when I walked to the podium. "Yes?" Strands of blond hair escaped from the bun on the back of her head.

"I'm listed for this flight," I said, showing her my driver's license. "What do you think my chances are?"

"Well, there are no other Non-Revs ahead of you, if that's any consolation but it is a full flight. There's another Detroit flight at ten o'clock."

"It's already overbooked," I said. "I checked the computer earlier."

"I don't know what to say. It all depends on how many show up. From the looks of things, you'll just have to wait and see."

"Thank you," I said and returned to my seat.

The morning of December 23rd I returned to our apartment from an early doctor appointment to find Clancy in bed, asleep. Elizabeth, his nurse, called to check on him.

"He's in a deep sleep," I said. "I can't rouse him."

Elizabeth arrived within fifteen minutes, accompanied by her supervisor. She took his pulse and listened to his heart. We both looked at the empty medicine bottles on the nightstand, saying nothing. She stayed in the apartment all day. I spent the time sitting next to the bed, talking to

Clancy. I told him I loved him and thanked him for loving me. Elizabeth came into the room around five o'clock as Clancy made a loud gurgling noise.

"It's the death rattle," she said.

Suddenly Clancy began to tremble with an intensity that lifted his arms right off the bed. Then the 5:15 Delta flight passed our bedroom window; Clancy turned his head. He opened his eyes, looked at me, smiled and stopped breathing. In aviation parlance, when a pilot dies, it's called "Flying West."

Janie was rummaging around in her carry-on. She pulled out a small blue bottle of Skyy vodka, removed the cap, tilted it to her mouth and greedily emptied the bottle. "That was good," she said. Her eyes flashed.

When my husband died and the men from the funeral home came for him, they wrapped him in a clean white sheet and placed his thin body on the gurney. There was no black plastic bag in sight. It was so sorrowful to see his tall athlete's body lifted as if it were light although I guess it probably was. They took him away in the elevator. I couldn't force myself to go with them.

I went out to the balcony and watched the men gently put him into the waiting white hearse. I went inside the apartment and wrote a letter to Dr. Donohue, his Mayo surgeon, telling him that Clancy had died. It was December 23rd and I have no idea how I spent the next 24 hours.

"Ladies and gentlemen," the gate agent announced over the P.A., "we're beginning the boarding process for Flight 999 to Detroit. This is a full flight and there are no standby seats available." A groan arced through the crowd. "Anyone needing extra time, or if you have small children, please go through Door F19 at this time." A lady with a walker and two men with canes hobbled down the jetway. "Now we are ready to board First Class, our Platinum, Gold and Silver customers and anyone seated in the exit rows."

Janie examined her ticket. "Oh, look, they put me in First Class on this flight too." She stood. "I hope you have a seat, Sheilah." She tottered away on the lizard boots, blowing me a kiss as she left.

The gate agent beckoned to me. "Go ahead. There's going to be an empty seat. We have one no-show. You take it," she said. "Hurry, they're going to close the door."

My route took me through the First Class cabin where I passed Janie, seated next to an attractive man. They were laughing as they enjoyed their drinks. Her face was flushed. She waved her fingers at me as I continued to Row 24, across from the bathroom. I wondered if he would call her after we landed.

"Listen, honey, come on out for dinner with me. It's been six months since he died. You've got to get out of that apartment".

"I can't, Billy. I just can't."

"Listen, I'll even wear my new Rolex for you."

"Billy, no thanks. I can't."

Later, in Detroit, my luggage was waiting for me at baggage claim. The Westin had a vacant room and the bed was soft and inviting. I caught the ten o'clock flight the next morning and returned to our silent apartment.

www.ingramcontent.com/pod-product-compliance
Lightning Source LLC
LaVergne TN
LVHW010943110826
845149LV00013B/2744
* 9 7 8 0 9 9 1 0 7 9 0 0 1 *